398.21
SAN

San Souci, Robert D.

The hired hand.

000029789
$15.89   07/16/1998

DATE			

THE HIRED HAND

An African-American Folktale

retold by ROBERT D. SAN SOUCI

pictures by JERRY PINKNEY

Dial Books for Young Readers   New York

Published by Dial Books for Young Readers
A Division of Penguin Books USA Inc.
375 Hudson Street
New York, New York 10014
Typography by Jane Byers Bierhorst
Printed in the U.S.A. on acid-free paper
First Edition
10 9 8 7 6 5 4 3 2 1

Library of Congress Cataloging in Publication Data
San Souci, Robert D.
The hired hand : an African-American folktale
retold by Robert D. San Souci
pictures by Jerry Pinkney.—1st ed.
p.   cm.
Summary: Old Sam hires a man to help out
at his sawmill, and the hired hand also teaches
Sam's lazy son a lesson about how to treat people.
ISBN 0-8037-1296-0 (trade).— ISBN 0-8037-1297-9 (lib. bdg.)
[1. Folklore, Afro-American. 2. Folklore—United States.]
I. Pinkney, Jerry, ill. II. Title.
PZ8.1.S227Hi 1997 [398.21]—dc20   93-36285   CIP   AC

*The full-color artwork was prepared
using pencil and watercolor.*

Special thanks to Kathie Meizner
of the Chevy Chase Community
Library in Chevy Chase, Maryland,
and to the Croton Free Library
in Croton-on-Hudson, New York
J. P.

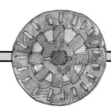

To Mike and Virginia
Mark, Shelley, Nick, and Robert George
Much love to all of you!

R.D.S.S.

To John Liney, cartoonist of Little Henry,
who in 1950 shared his magic
of drawing with me

J. P.

Down Virginia way, there once was a sawmill by a stream
at the edge of a forest. The stream turned a waterwheel that drove
a big saw that sliced logs into boards.

    The owner of the sawmill, Old Sam, was a hard worker and a
kind man. However, his son, Young Sam, didn't take after his pa.
He never cleaned dirt or stones from the logs before milling them,
so the saw blades got damaged. The boards he sawed were never
even. And he refused to sweep up the sawdust, saying, "Get some
hired hand to do that low work."

Old Sam would sigh. Then he'd repair the saw and even off the badly milled boards and sweep. His neighbors shook their heads and said, "That boy is a no 'count. He'll come to a bad end for certain."

One day in summer, along came a man who stood tall but looked as shabby as a worn-out shoe. "I want to learn saw-millin'," he said. "You teach me, an' I'll work a year for nothin'."

Old Sam was glad to get his help, and Young Sam saw a chance to shift some of his own work onto the New Hand. Old Sam always treated the New Hand politely, but his son put on airs, ordering him around like a servant, saying, "Do this" or "Do that."

The man never talked back; he just did what he was told.

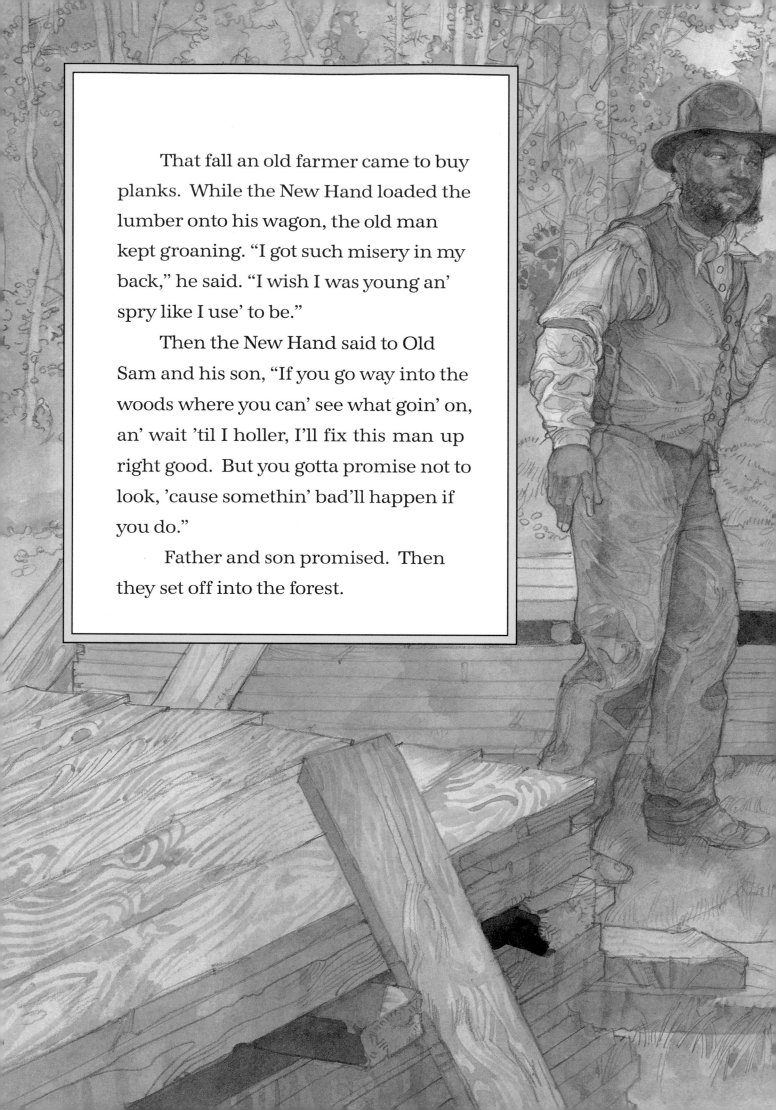

That fall an old farmer came to buy planks. While the New Hand loaded the lumber onto his wagon, the old man kept groaning. "I got such misery in my back," he said. "I wish I was young an' spry like I use' to be."

Then the New Hand said to Old Sam and his son, "If you go way into the woods where you can' see what goin' on, an' wait 'til I holler, I'll fix this man up right good. But you gotta promise not to look, 'cause somethin' bad'll happen if you do."

Father and son promised. Then they set off into the forest.

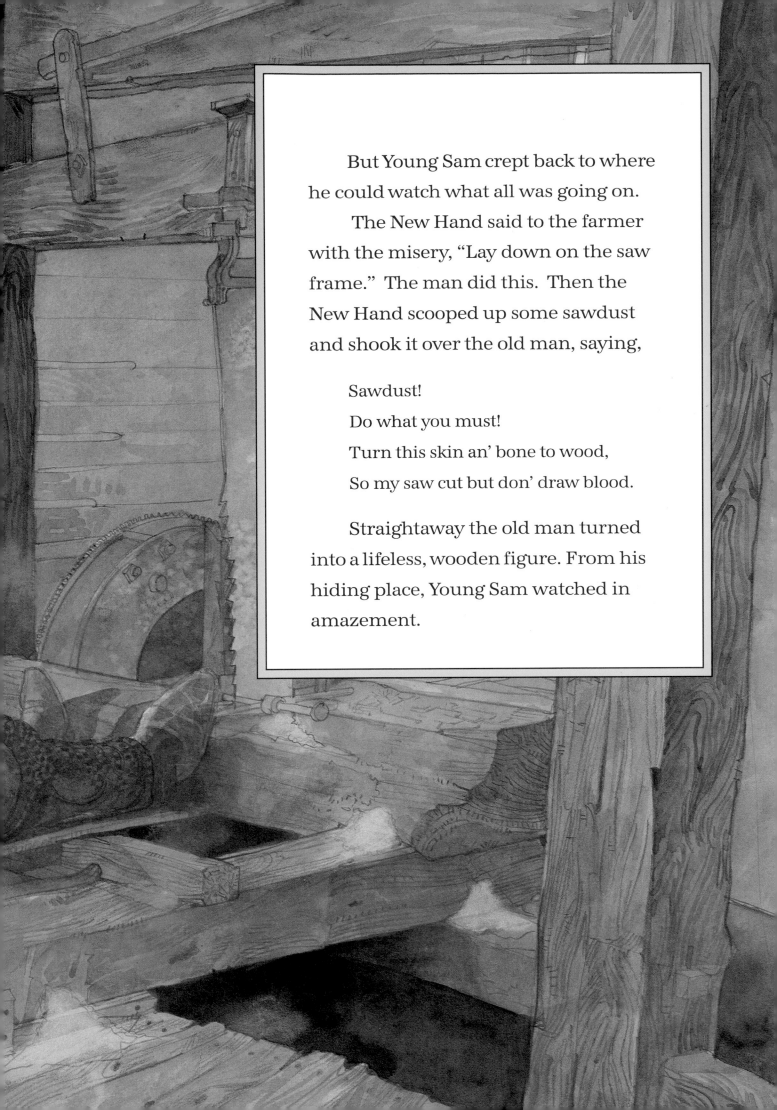

But Young Sam crept back to where he could watch what all was going on.

The New Hand said to the farmer with the misery, "Lay down on the saw frame." The man did this. Then the New Hand scooped up some sawdust and shook it over the old man, saying,

Sawdust!
Do what you must!
Turn this skin an' bone to wood,
So my saw cut but don' draw blood.

Straightaway the old man turned into a lifeless, wooden figure. From his hiding place, Young Sam watched in amazement.

Humming, the New Hand neatly sawed the wooden shape in half, then sawed each part in half again. He carried the four pieces to the stream. There he said,

> Water!
> Do what you oughtta!
> Wash misery from out this wood, an' then
> Make what cut up whole again.

All the while, he bathed the four wooden pieces with water. Then he put them together, like parts of a puzzle. Right away the pieces became whole again.

Finally the New Hand knelt beside
the wooden figure, jabbed his thumb
with a splinter, and drew a drop of blood.
Then he said,

Blood!
Do what you should!
When I touch these feet an' hands
   an' head,
You make come alive what dead.

He put a drop of blood on the wood-
en hands and feet and forehead, and life
came back into the old farmer. He sat up,
stretched himself like a sleeper waking,
and cried, "Great day in the morning!
My misery is gone!"

Then he looked in the stream, and saw that he was younger too. He clapped his hands and cried, "I feel frisky as a new calf! How can I thank you?"

The New Hand put his finger to his lips and said, "Just don' tell nobody how this happen'."

"I won'!" said the other man.

The New Hand cupped his hands around his mouth and hollered, "Sam an' Sam, you can come back now!" Though Young Sam had seen everything and overheard every word, he pretended to be just as surprised as his pa to see a young buck in place of the old man with the misery. Neither the New Hand nor the farmer would say what had happened.

But when the others had gone off, Young Sam said to the farmer, "That fellow work for Pa an' me. You got to pay or you won' be young no more."

So the man gave over all the gold he had. And Young Sam spent it on foolishness.

When winter chilled the countryside, Old Sam set out to visit a relative who lived far away. Before he left, he told his son, "Don' go gettin' high-handed with the new man, 'cause you're gonna need his help while I'm gone."

"I promise," said Young Sam.

But without Old Sam around, Young Sam wouldn't lift a finger. He put all the work on the hired man, then called him lazy and yelled at him to work faster. Finally the New Hand dropped an armful of lumber and said to Young Sam, "If you keep behavin' this way, I'm gonna leave tomorrow."

"Go 'long whenever you want!" Young Sam said. He didn't think the man would go. But the next day the New Hand was gone. "Now what I'm gonna do?" Young Sam wondered. "Someone gotta do the work, or we'll be broke 'fore Pa gets back."

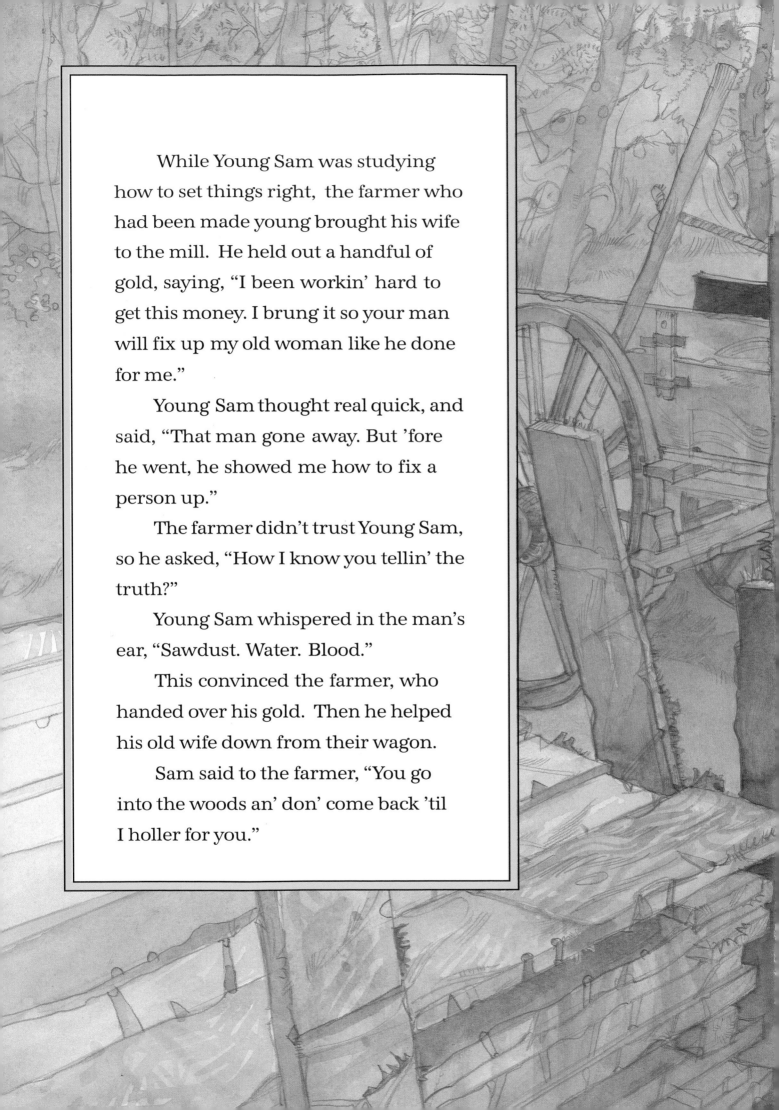

While Young Sam was studying how to set things right, the farmer who had been made young brought his wife to the mill. He held out a handful of gold, saying, "I been workin' hard to get this money. I brung it so your man will fix up my old woman like he done for me."

Young Sam thought real quick, and said, "That man gone away. But 'fore he went, he showed me how to fix a person up."

The farmer didn't trust Young Sam, so he asked, "How I know you tellin' the truth?"

Young Sam whispered in the man's ear, "Sawdust. Water. Blood."

This convinced the farmer, who handed over his gold. Then he helped his old wife down from their wagon.

Sam said to the farmer, "You go into the woods an' don' come back 'til I holler for you."

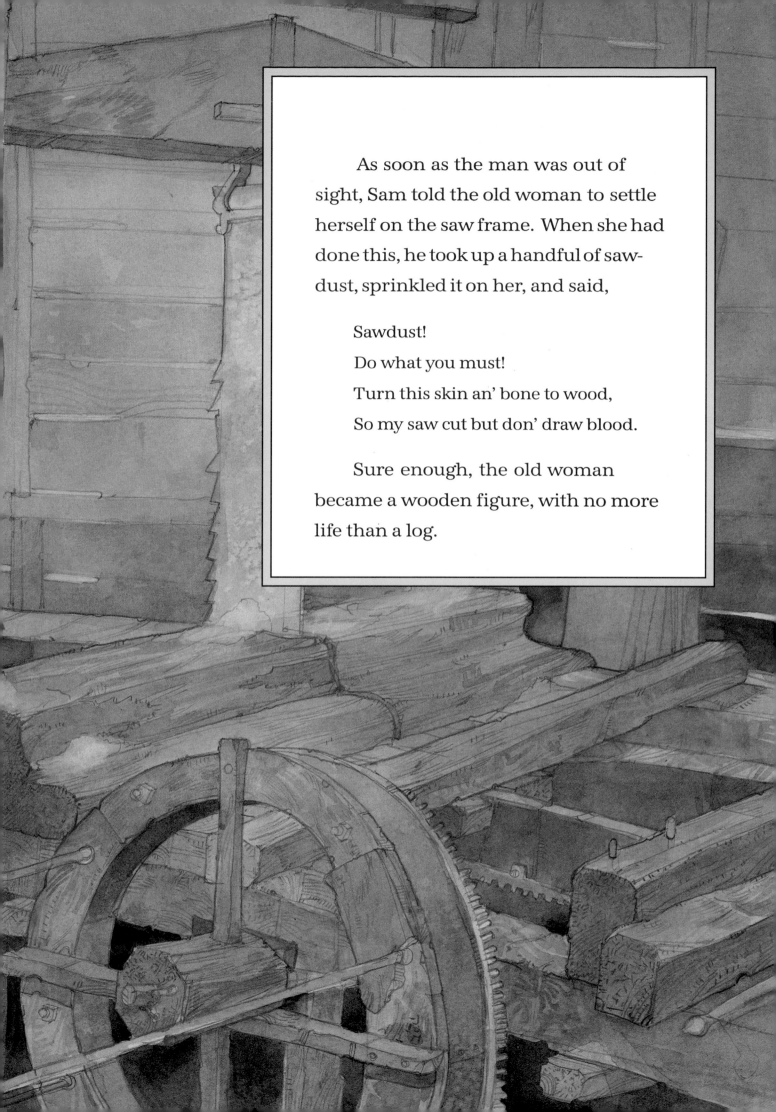

As soon as the man was out of sight, Sam told the old woman to settle herself on the saw frame. When she had done this, he took up a handful of sawdust, sprinkled it on her, and said,

Sawdust!
Do what you must!
Turn this skin an' bone to wood,
So my saw cut but don' draw blood.

Sure enough, the old woman became a wooden figure, with no more life than a log.

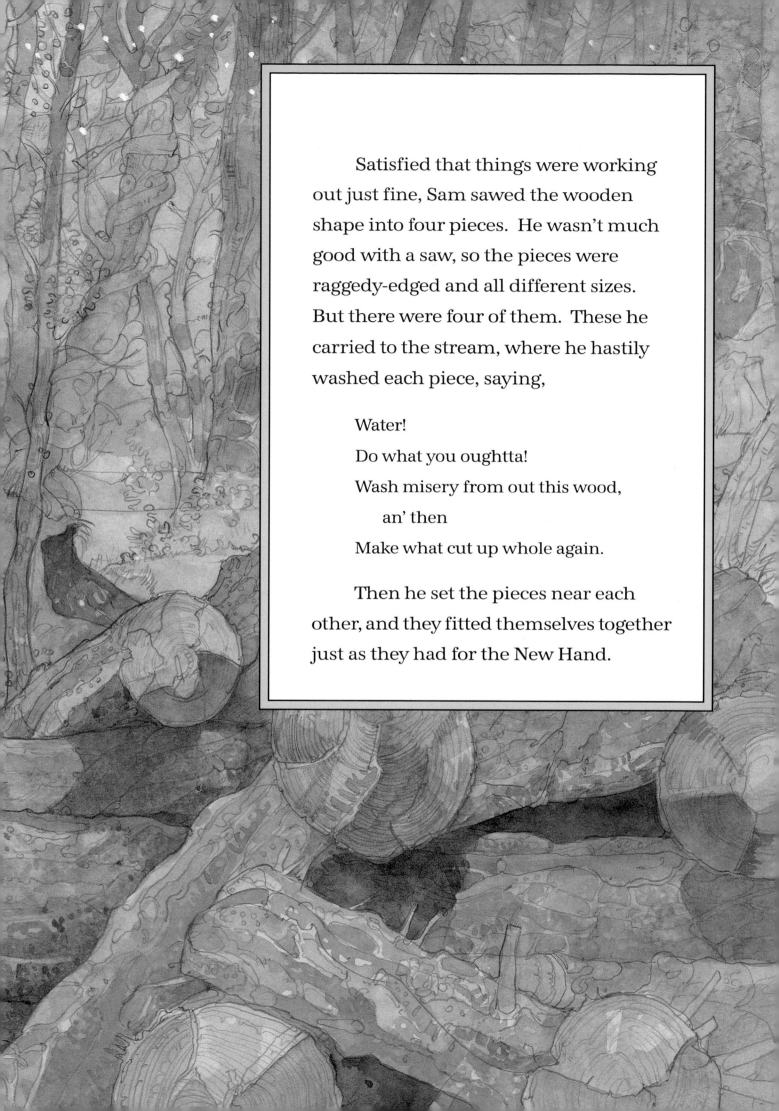

Satisfied that things were working out just fine, Sam sawed the wooden shape into four pieces. He wasn't much good with a saw, so the pieces were raggedy-edged and all different sizes. But there were four of them. These he carried to the stream, where he hastily washed each piece, saying,

Water!
Do what you oughtta!
Wash misery from out this wood,
   an' then
Make what cut up whole again.

Then he set the pieces near each other, and they fitted themselves together just as they had for the New Hand.

Pleased with himself, Sam got ready to finish. But the thought of sticking himself with a splinter and drawing a drop of blood made him feel faint. So he told himself, "Sawdust is sawdust, an' water is water. Any'll do. Guess it's the same for blood." So he took a dab of blood from a possum carcass hanging from a tree, and said,

> Blood!
> Do what you should!
> When I touch these feet an' hands an' head
> You make come alive what dead.

Well, the wooden figure was turned into a young woman. Only she was stone-cold dead.

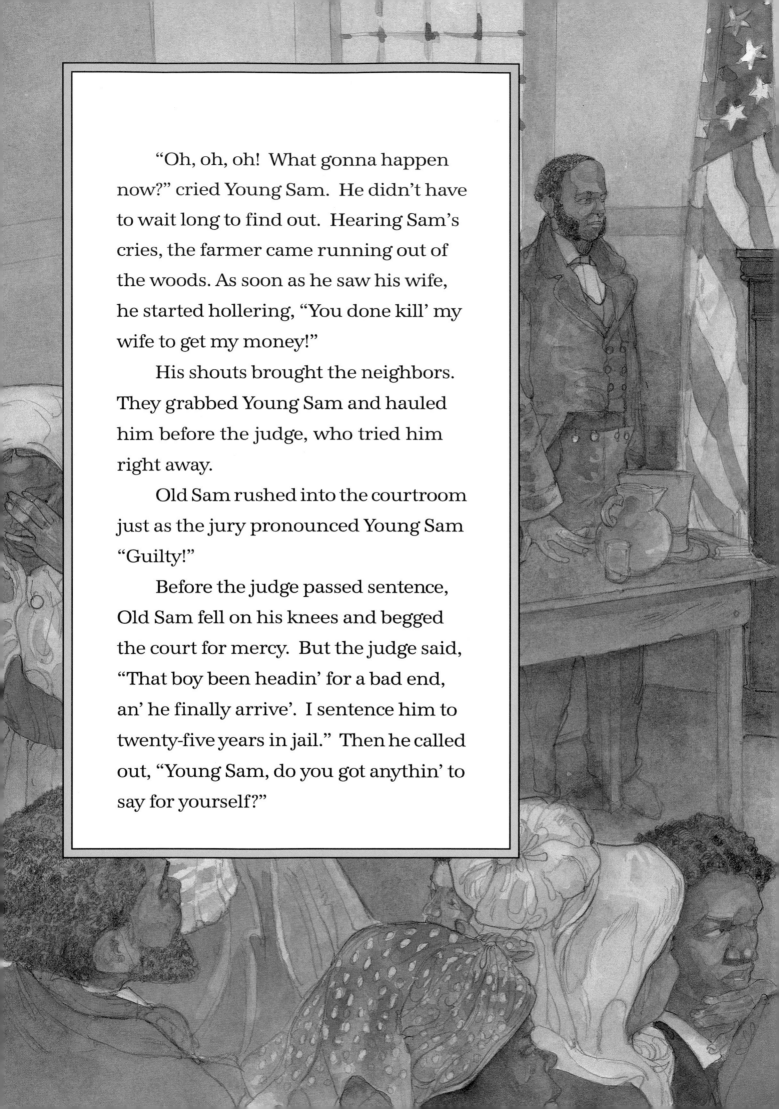

"Oh, oh, oh! What gonna happen now?" cried Young Sam. He didn't have to wait long to find out. Hearing Sam's cries, the farmer came running out of the woods. As soon as he saw his wife, he started hollering, "You done kill' my wife to get my money!"

His shouts brought the neighbors. They grabbed Young Sam and hauled him before the judge, who tried him right away.

Old Sam rushed into the courtroom just as the jury pronounced Young Sam "Guilty!"

Before the judge passed sentence, Old Sam fell on his knees and begged the court for mercy. But the judge said, "That boy been headin' for a bad end, an' he finally arrive'. I sentence him to twenty-five years in jail." Then he called out, "Young Sam, do you got anythin' to say for yourself?"

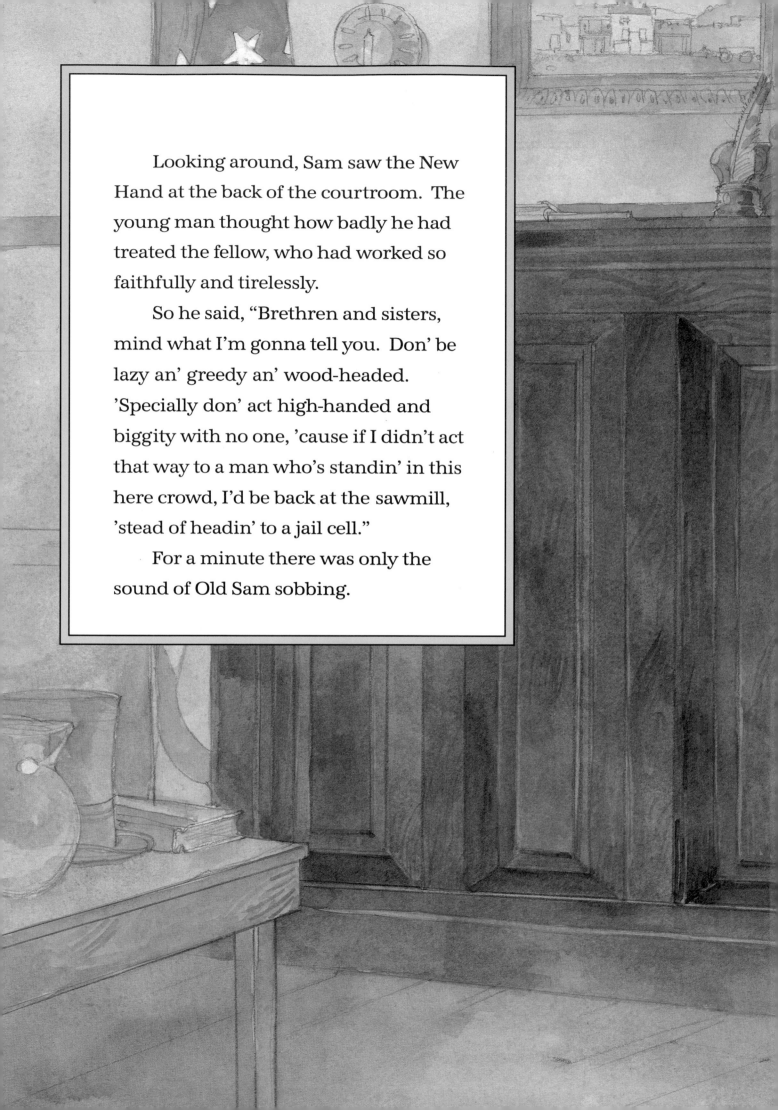

Looking around, Sam saw the New Hand at the back of the courtroom. The young man thought how badly he had treated the fellow, who had worked so faithfully and tirelessly.

So he said, "Brethren and sisters, mind what I'm gonna tell you. Don' be lazy an' greedy an' wood-headed. 'Specially don' act high-handed and biggity with no one, 'cause if I didn't act that way to a man who's standin' in this here crowd, I'd be back at the sawmill, 'stead of headin' to a jail cell."

For a minute there was only the sound of Old Sam sobbing.

Suddenly the New Hand marched to the front of the court-room, faced Sam, and asked him, "Are you sure enough sorry for what you done?"

Young Sam answered, "'Deed I am, an' I ax pardon an' hope you'll forgive me."

With that the New Hand loudly asked the court, "How come you gonna send this man to jail, when the woman you say he kill' is standin' right there?"

Everyone looked where he was pointing.

Sure enough, near the back door stood the farmer's wife—all young and pretty—beside her husband.

"Reconsiderin' the evidence," said the judge, "I find Young Sam not guilty."

Young Sam hugged his father, and they laughed and cried together. But when they turned to thank the New Hand, they couldn't find him in the crowd.

After this, Young Sam became the son that Old Sam had prayed he'd be. He worked from dawn to dusk, and the sawmill prospered as never before. They took on several hired hands, and Young Sam always treated them kindly and fairly.

But the New Hand was never seen in those parts again.

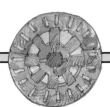

Author's Note

I chanced upon the original version of this story while reading *Gypsy Folk Tales* by Francis Hindes Groome (1851–1902). In this volume (published in 1899) folklorist Groome notes that a European Gypsy tale, "The Old Smith," is similar to a negro folktale "first printed by me in the *Athenaeum* for 20th August 1887." He adds that the tale "was taken down by an American acquaintance, in 1871, at Sand Mountain, Alabama, from the recitation of his negro servant, Dick Brown, a 'boy' about thirty years old, who was a native of Petersburg, Virginia, and there had got it from his granny."

Groome included the full text, entitled "De New Han'," as an appendix. It is a New World variant of a widespread folktale, including Greek and Roman versions. In its most familiar form the story involves slaying an aged person and boiling his or her bones in a cauldron to make him or her young again. Evildoers are destroyed either when they are tricked into letting themselves be slain in the hopes of being reborn—or when they reveal that they lack the power to make the cauldron return their victims to life.

In retelling the story I have tried to retain the flavor of the original, while softening the heavy use of dialect.

Artist's Note

I first thought that because this story took place at a black-owned sawmill in the slave state of Virginia, I would have to set it *after* the Emancipation Proclamation. But I wanted the story to have a real sense of *Once upon a time,* and with research, I came across a number of possible settings, including the mill town of Waterford, Virginia. Established in the early 1700's by antislavery Quakers, the town welcomed blacks. In fact, by the beginning of the next century one third of the people in Waterford were free black craftspeople. A town similar to that, I decided, would be a perfect setting for *The Hired Hand.*

I used the costumes from the eighteenth century to gain the element of visual magic I was looking for. I based my sawmill on the American water-powered ones from that century, but created the necessary world of make-believe with the influence of European fairy tale art. I knew that the farther back I set this story, the more magical it would become.

Mostly I wanted to provide a new, rich dimension to African-American folklore by bringing to the art a sense of time when free blacks were openly a part of several colonial communities, long before the Emancipation Proclamation.